A Big Fat Enormous Lie

by Marjorie Weinman Sharmat

illustrated by
David McPhail

A TRUMPET CLUB SPECIAL EDITION

Published by The Trumpet Club
666 Fifth Avenue, New York, New York 10103

ISBN 0-440-84664-1

This edition published by arrangement with Dutton Children's
Books, a division of Penguin Books USA Inc.

Printed in the United States of America
January 1993

Editor: Ann Durell
Designer: Meri Shardin

1 3 5 7 9 10 8 6 4 2
CUW

for my sons, Craig and Andrew,
with big fat enormous love

I told a lie.
A big fat enormous gigantic lie.
Father asked me if I ate the jar of cookies.
I said no.

But I did.
And I told a lie.
I could have told the truth.
I could have said "I ate the cookies."
But my father would have gotten mad

And my mother would have gotten mad.

And my sister.

Now I'm sorry I ate them.
And I'm sorry I lied.
And now I'm stuck with my lie.

I could talk to it, maybe.
"Lie, go away. Scram. I'll give you a dime
if you never come back."

It's still here.

"Look, Lie. I don't want you and I don't like you. And I can't see you, so maybe you don't exist. You don't exist, Lie. You are nothing. Nothing. Nothing. NOTHING!

So why are you still here?
I can't see you, but I know you're
getting bigger and bigger.
You are enormous, Lie."

"You are enormous and gigantic and you
are a big-fat. You have a mushy head

and a runny nose and a bulging stomach.
You are ugly, Lie."

"And dumb. You are the dumbest. I bet you can't spell your own name. Try it.

L-Y, L-I, L-Y-E, L-I-I-I, L-Y-Y-Y. All wrong."

"You are L-I-E, and you're dumb, and I'm

too smart for you. So how did I get
stuck with you?"

"Couldn't you go bother somebody else?
Somebody really mean and rotten. Not a
nice kid like me.

Is that you sitting on my stomach, Lie?
That hurts. Get off. Get off.
Okay, Lie. I give up."

"Father! Mother!

I lied to you. I know who ate the cookies.
Someone I like very much ate the cookies. He
sort of ate one and then he sort of ate another
and then he sort of ate another.
He sort of ate all the cookies in the jar."

"Yes. I sort of ate them. Me. Your son.

Are you going to do anything about it,
Father? Mother?"

"You two will discuss it?
Okay."
Okay!

My lie has gone. Maybe it left to bother
somebody else.

Maybe it's halfway around the world by now.
Maybe it's swimming in the ocean

or marooned on a beach waiting to be rescued.

Maybe it's lost in a big city

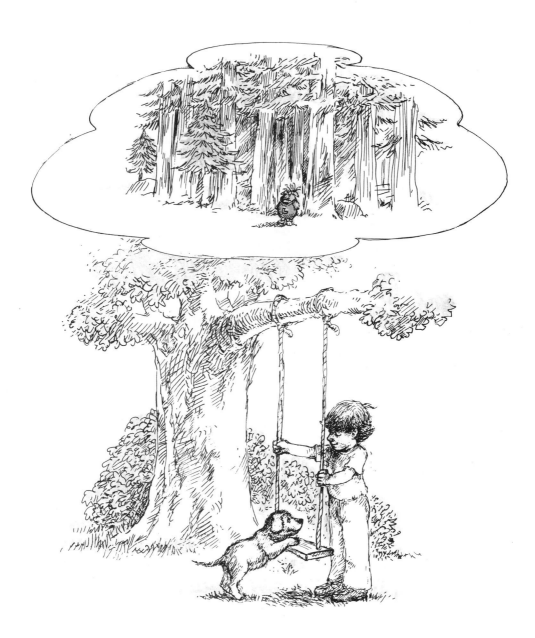

or a forest, wishing it hadn't left a
nice kid like me.
But it won't come back to me.
I don't have it anymore.

And that's the absolute and total truth.